The Bully Goat Grim

a Maynard Moose tale   as told to Willy Claflin   illustrated by James Stimson

AUGUST HOUSE
Little folk
ATLANTA

For Baby Troll!   --M.M.

For James   --W.C.

For Elise and Kira --J.S.

Text copyright © 2012 by Willy Claflin
Illustrations copyright © 2012 by James Stimson
All rights reserved. This book, or parts thereof, may not be
reproduced in any form without permission.

Book design by James Stimson
Audio CD recording, music, and voice-over introduction by Brian Claflin

Printed by Pacom Korea
Seoul, South Korea
April 2012

10 9 8 7 6 5 4 3 2 1

Published 2012 by August House LittleFolk
Atlanta, Georgia

augusthouse.com

LIBRARY OF CONGRESS CATALOGING-IN-PUBLICATION DATA

Claflin, Willy, 1944-
 The Bully Goat Grim : a Maynard Moose tale / as told to Willy Claflin ; illustrated by James Stimson.
     p. cm.
 Summary: A big bully, afflicted with Random Hostility Syndrome, terrorizes all of the forest animals until a clever young troll gets his goat.
 ISBN 978-0-87483-952-4 (hardcover : alk. paper)
 [1. Fairy tales. 2. Folklore--Norway.] I. Stimson, James, ill. II. Asbjørnsen, Peter Christen, 1812-1885. Tre bukkene Bruse. English. III. Title.
 PZ8.C498Bul 2012
 [E]--dc23
                           2012008626

The paper used in this publication meets the minimum requirements of the American National Standard for Information Sciences—Permanence of Paper for Printed Library Materials, ANSI Z39.48-1984.

AUGUST HOUSE, INC.
ATLANTA

Aroostook Moose Approved

Glossary and Hoofnotes
Moose Words and Their English Equivalents

Although this text has been painstakingly translated from the original Moose, it contains many traces of Piney Woods English, a dialect generally used by Aroostook County Mooses in northern Maine. Piney Woods words have been designated by hoofnotes in the form of *italics* in the text, and are defined below. We have also included a few special Grown-up Words (GW), of which northern moose are inordinately fond!

AMUNAL: animal, especially small furry animals of the Northern Piney Woods.

ANGRIFY: to make someone angry—very, very angry!

A-PO-GEE (GW): The highest point—where you stop going up, and start coming down.

BANDRIDGES: bandages.

BUSTERFLIES: piney woods butterflies; especially great big ones with bright white and gold wings, flapping happily amongst the wild blue bugleweeds.

DABUNDANCE: abundance; lots and lots and lots (and lots) of something.

DETENTION: attention.

DISPLAIN: explain, carefully and slowly.

DISTREMELY: extremely.

DOUBLE NEGATIVE (GW): Using two negatives together. Here's what Baby Troll says about that...... " 'Nobody better mess with him' means that nobody better mess with him. But 'Nobody better NOT mess with him' means you're SUPPOSED to mess with him. See? Like you're Not supposed to Not do it!"

DUBNOXIOUS: distremely obnoxious, like obnoxious times five! Yug!

E-CO-LO-GIS-TI-CAL HARMONIES: ecological harmony. Bertha is very smart—she has studied up on this. It means that all the amunals are supposed to get along and help each other, because they all live together in the same place. That makes sense, huh?

FAMBLY: family.

GADDUMP: to gallop with a sound of thundering hoofbeats! Yikes! Look out!

NEVER AFTERWORDS: A standard ending for Moose Tales. It means that the story is over, and there are no more words to say about that!

PROCESS (GW): talking stuff over, and over and over, and over and over again.

RANDOM HOSTILITY SYNDROME: A mental disorderation which makes one hostile, dubnoxious, violent, loathsome, dangerous, and angrified at everything, all the time. Yikes! Look out again!

SOPORIFIC (GW): Makes you sleepy. (Take a look at Beatrix Potter's Tale of the Flopsy Bunnies!)

SYNERGISTIC(GW): Working well together. Sometimes ideas work well together; sometimes they don't. Are three heads better than one? You might well ask yourself…

TRA-JEC-TO-REE (trajectory, GW): A curved path through the air. Whee!

TUBEROOT: A bulbous peppery root which grows deep in the heart of the Northern Piney Woods. If eaten in great quantity, it makes you twice more larger than normal.

UNCONSHABLE: Unconscious.

Far away in the Northern Piney Woods, there lives a storyteller named Maynard Moose. Every full moon in the forest, the animals come from near and far to hear him tell the old Mother Moose Tales, handed down so long ago. Young and old, big and small, fur and feather, the woodland creatures gather round and settle down on moss and branch and log to listen…

Did you ever walk out one fine and furry morning to sniff
the breeze, and hear the birdies go Twerp! Cheeple!,
when all of a sudden: Pow!
something would knock you down?
And you would be scared and run home and feel bad
and stare out the window and not know what to do?

Well, this is a story about that, and it goes like this.

Once upon a time,
there was a large and *dubnoxious* billy goat.
His name was Bully Goat Grim...

He was twice more larger than normal,
having bulked up in his youth on wild *tuberoot*,
which as you may understand, contains a
dabundance of natural steroids.
And so he grew to a large and ungainly size.

And as if that were not bad enough, he have a
distremely bad case of *Random Hostility
Syndrome*!

His favorite thing to do was whenever he would see a cute
little furry forest *amunal*, he would lower his big, boney Bully Goat head,

and *gaddump, gaddump, gaddump,*

gaddump,

Pow!

...over the tops of the trees would go sailing the hapless little furry mammal, and come crashing down in a pile of bracken on the other side. And pretty soon all the cute forest *amunals* had slings and crutches and *bandridges*!

Well, one morning when all the little bunnies and chipmunks and beavers and hamsters were bonked and bruised and hiding in their holes, the Bully Goat decide to go to the upland pastures, where he has heard that a wild variety of succulent mountain grasses grew in gay profusion.

Now the road to the upland pastures, it went over the river, and over the river there was a bridge, and under the bridge there lived a *fambly* of trolls.

There was a mommy troll with three heads, a daddy troll with two heads, and a little baby troll with only one head—but they loved her anyway. Because you should be grateful for what you are given! They were a happy little troll *fambly*...

they liked to wallow about in the mud down by the riverbank, and every Wednesday
they would go to the dump and bring home large and useless rusted and rotten objects.
And every night they would sit up late having rude noises contests, and they would all
sleep in the next morning.

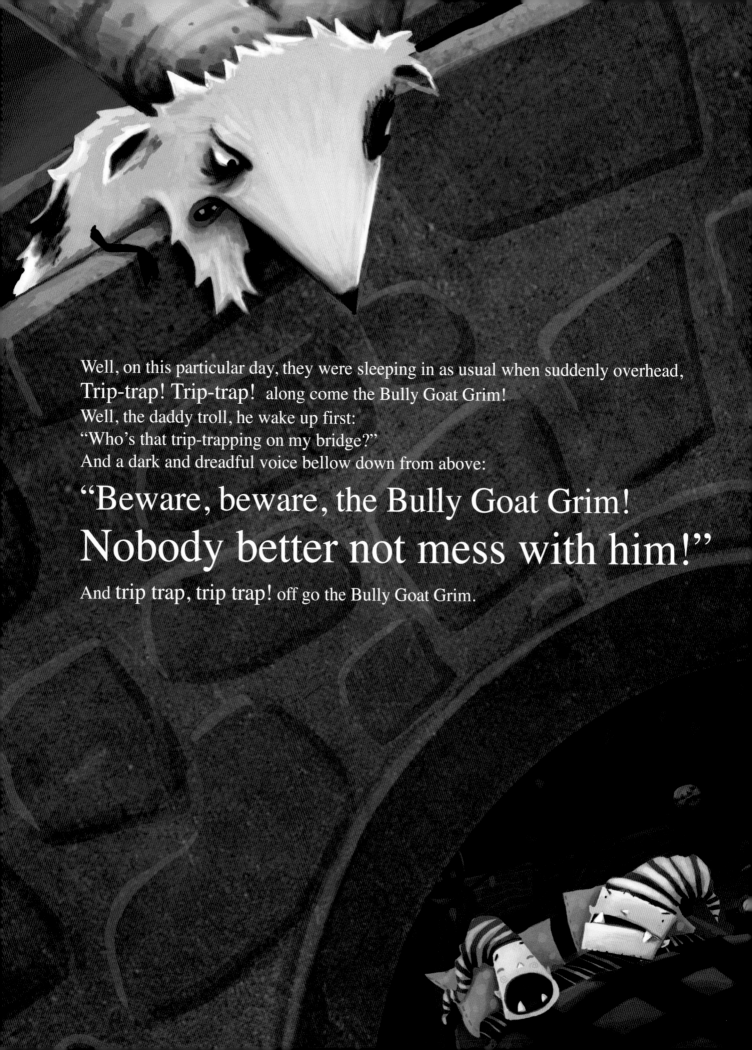

Well, on this particular day, they were sleeping in as usual when suddenly overhead, Trip-trap! Trip-trap! along come the Bully Goat Grim!

Well, the daddy troll, he wake up first:

"Who's that trip-trapping on my bridge?"

And a dark and dreadful voice bellow down from above:

"Beware, beware, the Bully Goat Grim! Nobody better not mess with him!"

And trip trap, trip trap! off go the Bully Goat Grim.

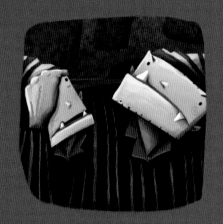

Now the daddy troll,
the head on the left, it spoke first:
"He do that again,
I gonna punch him in the nose!"

"You can't do that," say the right-hand head.
"That's a stupid idea."
"Who are you calling stupid?"
say the left-hand head.

"I just mean," say the right-hand head.
"With someone dangerous like the Bully Goat, you can't just
go punch him in the nose. You need a plan.
You can't just go and do something stupid like that."
"You call me stupid one more time,"
say the left hand head, "and I will mash your
nose out the back of your face."
"Oh yeah?" say the right-hand head.
"I'd like to see you try that."

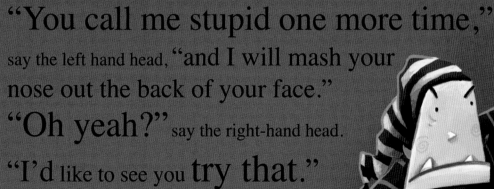

And before you know it—
a left! A right! Pow! Pow!
The daddy troll has knocked himself *unconshable*.
"You see that?" say the mommy to the baby troll.
"You better learn to get along with yourself.
Otherwise you'll wind up like your father,
unconshable as a muffin."

Well, the next morning, trip-trap! trip trap!, over the bridge come the
Bully Goat Grim. This time the mommy troll wake up first.
"Who's that trip-trapping on my bridge?" say the mommy troll.
And a dark and dreadful voice bellow down from above:

"Beware, beware, the Bully Goat Grim!
Nobody better not mess with him."

And trip-trap, trip-trap, off go the Bully Goat Grim.
Now, the mommy troll's heads were named Bertha, Gladys, and Louise.
"I think," said Bertha. "We should brew three cups of tea and assess the situation."
"Good idea," said Gladys and Louise...

"Now, I think," said Bertha, "if I may go first…" "Certainly," said Gladys and Louise. "And thank you for checking in about that." "I think," said Bertha, "that the Bully Goat is just acting out to get *detention*. I think we should *displain* to him that all the furry forest amunals are supposed to co-exist in *e-co-lo-gis-ti-cal harmonies*."

"Thank you," said Gladys. "Thank you for your proactive input. But I do not think the Bully Goat will listen to reason. I think we need to bake a big chocolate cake, and if he promise to be good, we give him the cake."

"Well," said Louise, "there is relative merit in both of your proposals, but I think he will listen neither to reason nor to bribery. I think we need to build a big trap door in the middle of the bridge. When the Bully Goat come, we pull on the rope, and splash! he go into the river below.

"Well," said Bertha, "Let us then take the best aspects of all three proposals, and in a *synergistic* fashion, combine them in order to…"

And so they talked on, and on, and on.
Until one by one, all three heads fell sound asleep.
(Because the effect of too much process is *soporific*.)

The next morning, once again--trip-trap, trip-trap, over the bridge come the
Bully Goat Grim. And this time the baby troll wake up first.
"Who's that trip-trapping on my bridge?" say the baby troll.
And once again, a dark and dreadful voice bellow down from above:

"Beware, beware, the Bully Goat Grim!
Nobody better not mess with him!"

And trip-trap, trip-trap, off go the Bully Goat Grim.

"Hmm…" say the baby troll. "Wait a minute! Nobody better Not…

Nobody better Not— That's a *double negative!*"

(Because she had been home-schooled by Bertha, Gladys and Louise.)

"If **nobody** better **not** mess with him,

that means… that **everybody** ought to mess with him!

So let's see, how can I mess with the Bully Goat?"

And all of a sudden,
a light bulb go on over her head!
"Look at that!" say baby troll.
"There's a light bulb over my head!

And look, there's a picture
of a pillow and a parachute!"

And so the baby troll get up and dig through the pile of trash and garbages

...and find herself a big fat moldy old pillow,

...and three raggedy old bedsheets for to sew together to make a parachute.

Early the next morning when the Bully Goat come trip-trapping along, the baby troll is waiting right there in the middle of the bridge, with the moldy old pillow strapped onto her behind, and the parachute on her back.

"Beware! Beware

the Bully Goat

Grim!

Nobody better not mess with him!"

bellow the Bully Goat.

But the baby troll put her thumbs in her ears and cross her eyes and wiggle her fingers, and make the rudest noise she knows how to make. Well, this *angrify* the Bully Goat Grim, and a thundercloud appeared over his head. He lower his big, boney, Bully Goat head; and gaddump, gaddump, gaddump, gaddump, across the bridge he come.

But at the last second, the baby troll turn around and stick her pillow behind up into the air, and POOF! Up into the air sail the baby troll! "Whee!"

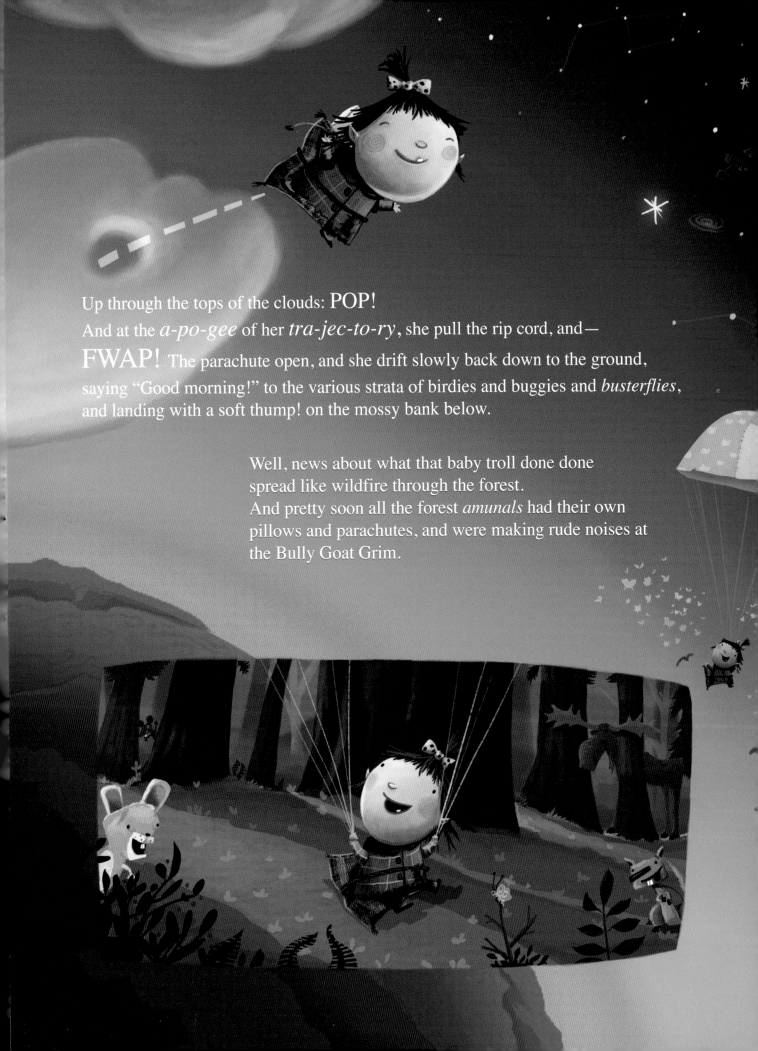

Up through the tops of the clouds: POP!

And at the *a-po-gee* of her *tra-jec-to-ry*, she pull the rip cord, and—

FWAP! The parachute open, and she drift slowly back down to the ground, saying "Good morning!" to the various strata of birdies and buggies and *busterflies*, and landing with a soft thump! on the mossy bank below.

Well, news about what that baby troll done done spread like wildfire through the forest.
And pretty soon all the forest *amunals* had their own pillows and parachutes, and were making rude noises at the Bully Goat Grim.

POOF! WHEEEEEEEEEEE!
Up into the air, over the tops of the trees would go sailing the happy
little furry *amunals*, drifting slowly down on the morning breeze,
saying Good Morning to the birdies and buggies and *busterflies*,
and landing with a soft thump! on the forest floor below.
And before long, they were lined up for miles, waiting for a free ride.
"My turn, Bully Goat! My turn!"

Now there is nothing worse than having *Random Hostility Syndrome* and not being able to injure anybody. It was *distremely* depressing to the Bully Goat Grim, and so finally he just give up and slunk away. He slunk, and slunk, and slunk, until he was completely away.

And the *amunals* took off their pillows and their parachutes,
and put them in the closet (just in case).

And the troll *fambly* went back to wallowing in the mud down by the riverbank.
And every Wednesday they went back to the dump, and brought home large and
useless rusted and rotten objects. And every night they sat up late having
rude noises contests, and they all slept in the next morning.

And they all lived happily for *never afterwords*!

Except for the Bully Goat.
He lived all by himself; alone and far away,
dubnoxiously for *never afterwords*.

So my advice to you is: keep a pillow and a parachute in your closet (just in case).

Learn to recognize a *double negative*!

And above all, *demember*—
nobody likes a *dubnoxious* beasty!

The end

↑ X' 0   cut Like ▽

Foot Pieces

↑ Sheet #1.